All the Seasons of the Year

By Deborah Lee Rose

Illustrated by Kay Chorao

Abrams Books for Young Readers

New York

The art in this
book was created using
gouache, colored pencils, and ink on
400 lb. hot-press watercolor paper.

Library of Congress Cataloging-in-Publication Data
Rose, Deborah Lee.
All the seasons of the year / by Deborah Lee Rose ; illustrated by Kay Chorao.
p. cm.
Summary: Describes in rhymed text how a mother cat's love for her kitten will last through the seasons of a lifetime.
ISBN 978-0-8109-8395-3
[1. Stories in rhyme. 2. Cats—Fiction. 3. Mother and child—Fiction. 4. Seasons—Fiction.] I. Chorao, Kay, ill. II. Title.
PZ8.3.R714Th 2010
[E]—dc22
2009039857

Printed and bound in China
10 9 8 7 6 5 4 3 2 1

Abrams Books for Young Readers are available at special discounts when purchased in quantity for premiums and
promotions as well as fundraising or educational use. Special editions can also be created to specification. For
details, contact specialmarkets@abramsbooks.com or the address below.

ABRAMS
THE ART OF BOOKS SINCE 1949
115 West 18th Street
New York, NY 10011
www.abramsbooks.com

To Susan Schulman, my friend through many seasons and books

—D. L. R.

For Sadie and Malcolm

—K. C.

I love you when autumn fills the sky—
when geese spread their wings and start to fly,
when trees wear a gold and scarlet crown
and leaves come gently drifting down,

when we rake them all up and jump right in
to feel their warmth against our skin.

$\mathcal{I}$ love you when the winter blows—
when wind chills our faces, fingers, toes,
when snowflakes glitter the quiet night
and morning greets us all in white,

and we pull on our gloves and race outside
to speed our sled on a downhill ride.

I love you when springtime breezes through—
when everything smells so sweet and new,
when crocuses pop and tulips flare
and daffodils are everywhere!

When we send up our kites and let them soar,
as if they've never been flown before.

I love you when the summer steams—
when snow and sleds are just in our dreams,
when the air is hot and full of bees
and leaves are thick in all the trees,

and we splash in the ocean and lake and pool,
flashing like fish in the watery cool.

I love you when fall is all ablaze—
when nights turn crisp and shorten the days,
when ducks look south across the pond
and lift off for places far beyond,

when we run through the grass in our favorite park,

then turn for home when it's almost dark.

I love you as the seasons flow—
and I can watch you change and grow.

I'll always love you, and hold you dear,
through all the seasons of the year.